Farmyard Tales

For Rob, Charlotte, Miranda, Amelia and Fred
In memory of Fiona
S.G.

For Gina and Murray
A.E.

ORCHARD BOOKS
96 Leonard Street, London EC2A 4RH
Orchard Books Australia
14 Mars Road, Lane Cove, NSW 2066
ISBN 1 86039 334 9
Text © Sally Grindley 1998
Illustrations © Andy Ellis 1998
The rights of Sally Grindley to be identified as the
author and Andy Ellis as the illustrator of this work
have been asserted by them in accordance with
the Copyright, Designs and Patents Act, 1988.
A CIP catalogue record for this book
is available from the British Library.
Printed in Dubai

Farmyard Tales

Sally Grindley

Illustrated by Andy Ellis

ORCHARD BOOKS

CONTENTS

Little Puddleditch Farm

Little Puddleditch Farm nestles into the side of a hill, with fields stretching away in front and woodland all around. Farmer and Mrs Larkin live there with their children, Daisy and Will, and a whole menagerie of animals. It is a noisy place, as you will discover.

Cosmo the Cockerel wakes everyone up in the morning: COCK-A-DOODLE-DOO! COCK-A-DOODLE-DOOO! WAKEY WAKEY!

The cows start to moo loudly:
MOOO! MOOOO!
They are ready to
be milked.
Gertie the Goat trots
into the farmyard, the bell round
her neck ringing loudly: JINGLE
JINGLE JINGLE. She's ready for
breakfast and eager for the
day to begin.
Primrose the Pig rolls over in
her sty. She wants a lie-in, but her
ten piglets jump to their feet,
squealing loudly: OINK! OINK! OINK!
They nuzzle against her tummy to
enjoy their morning milk. No peace for Primrose!
The hens in the hen-house watch for Mrs
Larkin to arrive with their food. CLUCK!
CLUCK! CLUCK! they go as they
chatter about the weather and
the fox and how many
eggs they have laid.

Farmer Larkin leaves the farmhouse and disappears into the cowshed, where the mooing grows louder – MOOOOOO, MOOOOOO, MOOOOOO! – milking machinery whirs – WHIRRRRRR – and buckets clank – CLANK CLANK.

Then Dancer the Donkey, out in his field, tells the world he's awake: HEE-HAW! HEE-HAW! HEE-HAW! He's waiting for his morning carrot.

Dabble and Dot the Ducks and their eight little ducklings go for an early morning swim in their pond – QUACK! QUACK! QUACK! PEEP! PEEP! PEEP! – and dive down for their breakfast of bugs and beetles.

When he has milked the cows, Farmer Larkin jumps into Little Red Tilly the Tractor and sets off across the farmyard – CHUG, CHUG, CHUG – to begin ploughing. Shoo the Sheepdog follows them, and rushes about barking wildly – RRRUFFF, RUFF, RRRUFFF! When the sheep have to be moved, Farmer Larkin blows his whistle: PEEEEE! Shoo barks instructions: WOOF! WOOF! And the sheep do as they are told (sometimes), complaining all the time: BAAA, BAAAA, BAAAAA, BAAAAAA!

Baggy the Bull is the last to wake up, in his field near the woods. BOOOO! BOOOO! He doesn't want anyone to forget him!

Every day begins the same on Little Puddleditch Farm. Well, nearly every day...

Baggy's Big Day Out

One morning Baggy the Bull felt very grumpy. He felt grumpy because he was bored. He was bored because he spent every day in the same field looking at the same grass and the same hedge. So he planned to escape.

Gertie the Goat was grazing in the next field. Baggy called her over.

"I want you to help me, please," he said.

"If it's naughty, I'll do it," said Gertie.

"I want you to open the gate to my field," said Baggy.

"That's naughty," said Gertie. "I'll do it."

She trotted over to the gate, pulled the metal bar with her teeth, and the gate swung open. Baggy lumbered out and looked around.

"It already looks better from this side of the gate. Now open the gate at the other end of your field. I want to visit the farm."

Gertie was only too happy to help Baggy. This was the naughtiest thing she had done for a long time.

"See you later," said Baggy, and off he ran.

He had never been in the farmyard before. There were all sorts of interesting smells and curious sounds. He came first to the hen-house. He bent down and peered in, expecting a friendly hello. But the hens all jumped in the air, squawking loudly: SQUAWK! SQUAWK! SQUAWK!

Funny lot, thought Baggy. Anyone would think they were frightened of me.

Next he came to the pigsty. He leant over and smiled at the ten little piglets. Primrose took one look at him and oinked loudly: OINK! OINK! OINK! Then she rushed to her piglets and pushed them into their pen.

Funny, thought Baggy. I was only being friendly.

When Crispin the Cat saw Baggy, he leapt up on a wall and spat: TTSSSS! When Shoo saw him he barked wildly: WOOF! WOOF! WOOF! and dashed into the farmhouse. Dancer began to bray: HEE-HAW! HEE-HAW! Cosmo began to crow: COCK-A-DOODLE-DOOOO! The sheep in their field and the cows in their stalls began to baa and moo: BAAA! BAAA! BAAAAA! MOO! MOO! MOOOOO!

When Baggy looked through the kitchen window, Mrs Larkin screamed: "AAAAAGH! The bull's got out!"

That was too much for Baggy. He panicked and ran across the farmyard. He trampled over Mrs Larkin's tomato plants, knocked over Daisy Larkin's climbing frame, flattened Farmer Larkin's raspberry canes and pulled down the washing line. Now he couldn't see. Will Larkin's dungarees hung from his horns across his eyes.

Baggy shook his head, kicked out his legs, and trod in Gertie's lunch. He snorted frantically. This was meant to be a fun day out. Some fun!

At last the dungarees fell down and Baggy could see where he was. Farmer Larkin was coming towards him with a long piece of rope. Baggy didn't wait to see what the rope was for. He had had enough. He was off, out of the farmyard, past the pigsty, past the hen-house, past the barns, across Gertie's field and into his own.

"Shut me in, please," he begged Gertie. "I think I prefer my field after all!"

Hetty and the Champion Egg Layer

The hen-house was a happy place, until Hyacinth arrived.

When Hyacinth arrived, Hetty and the other hens clucked around excitedly. But Hyacinth put her wing across her eyes and said, "Leave me alone. I am a champion egg layer. I must have peace and quiet." With that she tottered across the hen-house and sat herself down – in Hetty's nesting box.

Hetty's beak dropped open. "Er, excuse me," she said. "I wonder if you wouldn't mind moving to that box over there, only this box is mine and that one's empty."

"Oh, I couldn't possibly move," said Hyacinth. "I am feeling ill, and besides, I wish to be by a window. I am sure you will agree a champion egg layer must have the best. Why don't you have the empty box?"

Hetty couldn't believe her ears. She had always had the same nesting box. All the hens had their own nesting boxes. She was about to protest when Hyacinth interrupted.

"I don't wish to talk about it any more. I have had a long, tiring day and I am going to sleep." She turned her back and closed her eyes.

Hetty and the other hens were speechless. They trooped out of the hen-house and huddled together.

"What am I going to do?" wailed Hetty.

"What are *we* going to do?" said Harriet. "We can't just let a newcomer push us around."

"When she gets up from your box, we'll grab it back for you," said Hilda.

But Hyacinth didn't get up for the rest of that day. When night fell and it was time to settle down, Hetty tried to make herself comfortable in the empty box. She scratched around and shifted the straw and tried all sorts of different positions, but it just wasn't the same as her own box.

Next morning Hyacinth stood up and said, "Well, I had an awful night's sleep. This box is nowhere near as comfortable as the one I had at my last house, and I could hear the fox scratching around outside. It's just not good enough for a champion egg layer."

"Perhaps you'd like to try this box then," said Hetty, "and let me have my box back."

"No," said Hyacinth. "I shall stay here and make the most of it, though I am not at all happy."

Hetty wasn't at all happy either. She and the other hens wandered out into the yard again.

"What do we do now?" Hetty squawked.

"Don't worry," said Harriet. "Hyacinth will have to get up to eat sooner or later. When she does, we'll all rush inside and close the door behind us. We won't let her back in unless she keeps out of our boxes."

It was lunchtime before Hyacinth strutted out into the yard.

"I hope you have left me some food," she said. "As a champion egg layer I need to keep up my strength."

The other hens waited until she was well away from the hen-house, then they dashed inside, and leant against the door. When Hyacinth came back, she pushed the door but it wouldn't open.

"Let me in," she said.
"I shall catch a cold
out here."

"You can only come in
if you promise to keep out
of our boxes," said Hilda.

"Don't be so ridiculous,"
said Hyacinth. "I am a champion egg layer.
I must have the best. Now let me in."

The hens were determined not to let Hyacinth
in until she promised. Hyacinth wouldn't
promise. So that night the hens slept inside the
hen-house pressed up against the door while
Hyacinth stayed outside.

But it was cold outside, the ground was uncomfortable and there were strange noises. And then the fox came prowling.

Hyacinth heard his creeping paws – SQUAWK! – saw his steamy breath – SQUAWK! – saw his hungry eyes looking at her – SQUAWK! SQUAWK! He was coming after her. She was so frightened she couldn't move.

Inside the hen-house Hetty couldn't sleep. She peered through the window and saw the fox creeping closer and closer to Hyacinth. She pushed the sleeping hens out of the way and pulled open the door. She rushed out, grabbed Hyacinth by the tail and dragged her into the hen-house just in time.

Hyacinth collapsed into Hetty's wings. "Oh, thank you," she sobbed. "You saved my life."

From that day onwards Hyacinth changed. She still boasted about her egg laying, but then she was very good at it. But she made herself at home in the empty box and never again expected to be treated differently.

Scarecrow Scared and a Pocketful of Warmth

Scarecrow Scared couldn't scare a crow to save his life. He couldn't even scare the tiniest wren or the cheekiest bluetit.

Daisy, Will and Farmer Larkin had made Scarecrow Scared from piles of straw and buttons and old clothing. They carried him out to the field where Farmer Larkin had sown seeds for corn.

"Make sure you scare away those birds or

they'll eat up my seeds," said Farmer Larkin as they walked away. Scarecrow Scared nodded in the wind, but under his coat his heart beat faster and his tummy filled with butterflies.

"Don't leave me, I'm scared of birds," he whispered through the air, but Farmer Larkin couldn't hear him.

Scarecrow Scared stood with his arms out wide and peered nervously across the field. Suddenly, two crows flew in.

Oh no! What do I do? thought Scarecrow Scared. The crows began to peck at the seeds.

"Go away," he whispered. "Please go away."

The crows took no notice and stalked towards him, eating all the way.

"CAW! CAW!" crowed the crows. "Scare us off then, do your job."

"Shoo," said Scarecrow Scared. "Shoo, shoo."

But the crows just laughed, "HAW! HAW!" One of them jumped on top of Scarecrow Scared's hat.

Scarecrow Scared's knees quivered and his arms shook and he hunched his head into his shoulders and said, "Please leave me alone."

"Scared of crows, scared of crows, this scarecrow here is scared of crows," chanted the crows.

Three crows who were perched on a nearby tree joined the others, and it wasn't long before crows flew in from all directions. As soon as they heard that Scarecrow Scared was too scared to stop them, they tucked in to a feast of seeds. Scarecrow Scared hung his head in shame.

When Farmer Larkin saw the crows all over his field, he tutted crossly. He pulled Scarecrow Scared up and carried him back to the barn, where he slung him into a corner. Scarecrow Scared lay there for days, feeling worthless and unloved.

Then, one sunny morning, a little bird came in.
"Hello, Scarecrow," she said.

Scarecrow Scared was too scared to answer.
He watched her nervously as she hopped
here and there.

"I'm looking for just the right place," she said.
Scarecrow Scared frowned
nervously when the little bird
jumped onto his leg and then
into his pocket.

"This will do fine," she said.
He giggled nervously when
she pulled pieces of straw
from his arm, because
it tickled.

"I didn't hurt you, did I?" she said.
The little bird stuffed the straw into his pocket.
She pulled some cotton from his coat and put that
in the pocket too.

"I hope you don't mind," she said.

Scarecrow Scared was too scared to ask what
she was doing, but he grew used to her comings

and goings and began to look forward to seeing her. He was amazed when at last she settled down in his pocket and sat there quietly day after day. He could feel her warm body and it made him feel warm inside.

He was woken one morning by a loud CHEEP! CHEEP! CHEEP! The little bird hopped out of his pocket and said, "Morning, Scarecrow. Will you look after my babies for me while I find some food?" Scarecrow Scared nodded shyly and the little bird flew off.

The CHEEP! CHEEP! CHEEP! grew louder and louder. Scarecrow Scared peered down at his pocket and saw three tiny bald heads with great big yellow beaks squealing for food.

"Don't worry," he said to
them gently, "your mummy will
be back soon. I'll keep you safe."
Scarecrow Scared felt wanted at
last. All through the spring the little
wren flew to and from his pocket to
feed her babies. While she was away,
Scarecrow Scared looked after them. Then
it was time for the babies to leave their nest.
One by one, they wriggled from his pocket,
chirping merrily, and hopped all over him.

He giggled because it tickled; he chuckled because they looked funny; he laughed because he was happy.

He watched them as they learned to fly, until the day came when they were ready to leave. The little wren hopped onto his leg, then onto his arm and up onto his shoulder. She whispered in his ear, "Scarecrow, can I come back again next year? You're the best babysitter in the world."

Scarecrow Scared nodded his head and smiled. What did it matter that he couldn't scare crows?

Primrose and the Missing Piglet

Primrose the Pig was a very happy pig indeed. She was the mother of ten fat little piglets. She didn't mind that they trampled all over her. She didn't mind that they wore her out with their feeding and playing. She didn't mind that they wouldn't let her sleep. They were her pride and joy.

"Just look at my piglets," she said to the other animals whenever they passed by her sty.

"That little one's got a naughty face," said Gertie the Goat. "He'll cause you no end of worry."

Primrose was shocked. "What can you mean, Gertie? All my piglets are as good as gold. There's not an ounce of naughtiness in them."

"You'd be surprised," said Gertie, and she trotted off.

What does she know, thought Primrose to herself, and she gathered her piglets round her. The little one, Perky, didn't come straightaway. He was too busy exploring the sty.

"Coming, Mum," he squeaked when she called him for the third time.

"You must come straightaway when I call you, my little pumpkin," Primrose said, fondly.

"Yes, Mum," squeaked Perky. "Can we play hide-and-seek after lunch?"

"Yes, of course we can, my little dumpling."

After lunch Mrs Larkin arrived to change their straw.

"Can we play hide-and-seek now?" squeaked Perky to his mother.

"Of course, my little cherub," said Primrose.

"I'll hide first," squeaked Perky.

Primrose and her nine piglets closed their eyes. Perky waited until Mrs Larkin was looking the other way, then made a dive for the open gate and was off across the farmyard. Mrs Larkin closed the gate and went back to the farmhouse.

"Are you ready, my little blossom?" said Primrose.

There was no reply. Primrose and the piglets opened their eyes and began to search the sty. They peered under the food trough, they looked behind the pen, they rummaged through the pile of straw, but there was no sign of Perky anywhere.

"Come out, come out wherever you are, my little sugarplum," said Primrose, who was beginning to worry. She went over to the gate and saw Gertie munching near by.

"Gertie, oh Gertie, I've lost my littlest roly-poly. He may have wandered out of the sty and he'll be so frightened out there."

"I told you he was a naughty one," said Gertie. She called all the other animals round her. "We're missing a piglet," she said. "We must all help to find him."

"He's my littlest wriggly-pie," said Primrose, "and he'll be *sooooo* frightened without his mummy." She burst into tears and her nine piglets snuggled up close to comfort her.

The animals set off round the farm. Shoo the Sheepdog looked in the stable, but Perky wasn't there. Crispin the Cat looked in the barn, but he wasn't there.

Dancer the Donkey looked in the garden, but he wasn't there. Gertie hoped he hadn't fallen in the duck pond, but Dabble the Duck hadn't seen him. Hyacinth the Hen found it all too tiring and went into the hen-house for a rest. Suddenly, an enormous squawk stopped the other animals in their tracks. Hyacinth flew out of the hen-house, flapping her wings hysterically.

"The pig's in my nest box!" she squawked. "In my nest box! Oh, this is too much for a champion egg layer to bear."

"Don't be so silly," said Hetty the Hen. She brushed past Hyacinth while the other animals crowded round outside. There, half hidden in the straw, was Perky, fast asleep. Hetty prodded him with her wing and he woke with a start.

"Found you," said Hetty. "Your mum's been looking for you everywhere."

"Is she cross?" squeaked Perky.

"She's very worried," said Hetty. "It's naughty to go off without telling her. What if something happened to you?"

"I just wanted to hide somewhere different," squeaked Perky.

Gertie led Perky back to the sty. When Primrose saw her missing piglet she burst into tears again and hugged him tight.

42

"Oh, my little pumpkin, dumpling, cherub, blossom, sugarplum, roly-poly, wriggly-pie, I've missed you *sooooo* much. Are you all right, my little poppet?"

"Yes, Mum," squeaked Perky. "I'm sorry I made you worry."

"You were a teeny bit naughty this time, my little pumpernickel, but I know you won't be again," said Primrose.

"No, Mum, I won't," squeaked Perky.

Primrose and her ten piglets settled down for their afternoon nap. Gertie smiled a knowing smile and went back to her munching.

Dabble and Dot and the Vanishing Pond

The duck pond was small and round and hidden from the farmyard by bushes and tall reeds. It was home to Dabble and Dot the Ducks and their eight little ducklings.

One hot, sunny day Dabble said to Dot, "Our pond is getting smaller."

"How do you know, dearest?" asked Dot.

"It used to take one hundred and twenty paddles of my feet to swim across it. Now it only takes one hundred. Someone must be stealing our water."

"Oh, but why would anyone do that?" asked Dot.

Dabble didn't know, but he was determined to find out. "We'll take it in turns to sit on our nest and keep watch," he said.

The two ducks kept watch in the sweltering heat all through the following week. Nobody came. But when Dabble next swam across the pond to find out how big it was, he let out a loud QUACK! QUACK! QUACK!

"It's even smaller!" he cried. "It's only ninety paddles!"

"Perhaps there's a hole in the bottom," said Dot.

Dabble dived down to look, but there was no hole. "It's vanishing before our very eyes," he said. "We need help."

The ducks left their nest and waddled into the farmyard.

"Hi, quackers," said Shoo the Sheepdog. "Going for a stroll?"

"Someone is stealing our pond," said Dabble. "We need help to find out who it is."

Primrose the Pig stood up at the wall of her sty. "Perhaps the fish are drinking it," she said. "It's very thirsty weather at the moment."

"Perhaps the frogs are splashing too much," said Shoo.

"Nonsense," said Gertie the Goat, who had been listening. "The sun is stealing your pond, you mark my words."

"How can the sun steal our pond?" asked Dabble.

"It magics it up into the air, drop by drop, and carries it away," said Gertie.

"How can we stop it?" asked Dot.

"You can't," said Gertie. "You'll just have to wait until it rains. The sun doesn't like the rain."

Day after day, Dabble and Dot waited for rain, but the rain stayed away. The pond grew smaller and smaller. The other animals tried to help.

"Here's some water," said Dancer the Donkey, tipping in a bucketful.

Shoo brought his water bowl. "I had to drink some of it, but there's a little left," he said, tipping in a drop.

Gertie turned on the hose, but it wasn't long enough to reach the pond.

The pond went on shrinking. The ducklings waddled into the farmyard to find water. Three of them took turns to splash around under a dripping tap. Two of them toddled into the kitchen and jumped in and out of Crispin the Cat's water bowl. The other three had so much fun chasing the chicks round the hen-house that they forgot all about their vanishing pond.

At last, Dabble and Dot decided that they would have to find a bigger pond.

"We'll have to leave Little Puddleditch Farm, I'm afraid," said Dot.

One by one, the animals came to say goodbye. That night, the ducks and their ducklings wrapped their wings round each other and cried themselves to sleep.

In the middle of the night, Dabble was woken by something hitting him on the bill. PLIP.

"What was that?" he quacked, indignantly. Then something hit him on the tail. PLOP. "Stop it," he said. Then something hit him on his head and his back and his wings. PLIP PLOP PLIP PLOP. He looked up through the reeds and a plop of water hit him right in the eye. "OUCH!" Dabble shook himself and flapped his wings excitedly.

"It's raining!" he cried, waking Dot and the ducklings.

Dabble rushed into the farmyard and woke the other animals. "It's raining, it's raining! We might not have to leave after all."

The ducks watched day after day as the rain fell, drop after drop, in their pond. Dabble counted how many paddles of his feet it took to swim across. Sixty, eighty, one hundred. Their pond was coming back.

Just let the sun try and steal it again!

Little Red Tilly Finds a Friend

Little Red Tilly the Tractor was getting old. Her paint was peeling, her joints were creaking and her engine was rusting. She had worked at Little Puddleditch Farm for twenty-five years and all the animals loved her.

One day Farmer Larkin drove a new tractor into the farmyard. The animals couldn't believe their eyes.

"What's *he* doing here?" said Shoo the Sheepdog.

"Looks like he's come to do Little Red Tilly's work," said Gertie the Goat.

"Poor Little Red Tilly will be *soooo* upset when she sees another tractor on her farm," said Primrose the Pig.

They found Little Red Tilly peering through the doors of her barn.

"He's big," said Little Red Tilly. "I expect he's quick and strong. It hurts my engine when I pull heavy loads, and I find the hills very tiring."

"We don't want him here," said Shoo.

"I'm sure you'll like him," said Little Red Tilly. But she looked so sad that the animals decided to make life very difficult for the new tractor. Then perhaps he would go away.

They went back into the farmyard just as Farmer Larkin was climbing back into the tractor's cab.

"Come on, Big Blue Turbo," he said, "show me what you can do."

Big Blue Turbo's engines roared into life: BRRRRM, BRRRRM! He thundered across the farmyard, splattering the animals with mud.

"I'm very sorry," he said.

"You did that on purpose," screamed Gertie after him, but he didn't hear.

Over the next few days, the animals did everything they could to stop Big Blue Turbo from doing his work so that Farmer Larkin would send him away. They ran in front of him so that he would have to stop suddenly, throwing Farmer Larkin out of his seat. They made as much noise as they could when he was resting – BAA! WOOF! OINK! MEOW! CLUCK! QUACK! HEE-HAW! – to make him too tired to work.

When he spoke to them they ignored him or told him he wasn't wanted.

In the barn at night, Big Blue Turbo said to Little Red Tilly, "The animals don't seem to like me. I've tried very hard to be nice to them, but I think they want to get rid of me."

"Oh dear," said Little Red Tilly. "It's my fault. The animals are upset because you are doing my work."

"They are right to be upset then," said Big Blue Turbo. "I don't want to take your work."

"My paint is peeling, my joints are creaking and my engine is rusting," said Little Red Tilly. "I don't want to do the work any more, but I don't want to sit around doing nothing."

In the morning, Little Red Tilly asked Hetty the Hen to bring the animals to see her. Hetty ran across the farmyard and over to the field where Big Blue Turbo would soon begin harvesting. She arrived to find Gertie loosening his handbrake and shouting "NOW!" to Baggy the Bull and Dancer the Donkey.

"Please don't," cried Big Blue Turbo. "I'll lose my job."

Baggy and Dancer and all the other animals ignored him as they pushed and pushed and pushed – HEAVE! – until Big Blue Turbo began to move. Gertie turned his steering wheel and, suddenly, his left wheels plunged downwards – WHOOOAA! – and he fell into a ditch.

Farmer Larkin's angry voice bellowed across the farmyard: "What's going on?" – and the animals ran off in all directions.

Little Red Tilly was shocked when she heard them squealing, "Big Blue Turbo's in the ditch, Big Blue Turbo's in the ditch!"

"But that's awful," she said when they told her what had happened.

"He deserved it," said Shoo. "He's taken your work from you."

"He's only doing what he's been asked," said Little Red Tilly. "Besides, I don't want to do that work any more. I'm too old."

Just then Farmer Larkin came into the barn.

"Come on, Little Red Tilly," he said. "I've got a big job for you."

He drove Little Red Tilly over to where Big Blue Turbo was stuck fast in the ditch. He tied ropes to her back and to the front of Big Blue Turbo, then he ordered her to pull as hard as she could. Little Red Tilly pulled and pulled – HEAVE, HEAVE – until Big Blue Turbo's wheels found a grip on the ground and thundered into action.

"Well done, Little Red Tilly," said Farmer
Larkin. "You're still one of the pluckiest tractors
I know."

Little Red Tilly sat in the field and watched as
Big Blue Turbo set off to work. Then she looked at
the animals and smiled.

"He's big, he's quick, he's strong, and he's my
friend. I want him to stay here."

The animals nodded. If Little Red Tilly could be
friends with Big Blue Turbo, then so could they.

"And now," said Little Red Tilly, "I'm going to
have a rest. All that pulling has tired me out."

There was still plenty for Little Red Tilly to do. In the warm months, Farmer Larkin kept her busy towing trailers full of children round the farm. Sometimes she helped to move the animals from one part of the farm to the other. She loved her new work, but she also enjoyed the days when she could simply rest in the sunshine and watch the world go by.

Shoo and the Silly Sheep

Shoo the Sheepdog was very young but he had a very important job. He helped Farmer Larkin move his sheep from one field to another, or into the barn. Shoo loved his job. When Farmer Larkin whistled, Shoo crouched down low, ran this way and that way and crept round in circles. Shoo thought he was very good at his job. Farmer Larkin said he had a lot to learn.

The trouble was, the sheep kept escaping and that made Farmer Larkin cross. "You'll never be a good sheepdog if you don't pay attention," he said.

"I only turned away once when I saw a very pretty butterfly," said Shoo to Baggy the Bull. "And I only chased one rabbit, and I only looked down one rabbit hole, and I only went to speak to Gertie the Goat once. It's the sheep who aren't very good."

One day Shoo decided to prove that he was a good sheepdog. "I'm going to lead them from the field over to the barn all on my own. Won't Farmer Larkin be surprised?" he said to Baggy.

Straight after lunch, when Farmer Larkin was busy with Big Blue Turbo, Shoo ran over to the sheep field.

"Now listen to me, you silly sheep. It's time to go over to the barn. Farmer Larkin is busy, so I'm in charge. Just you do exactly as I tell you."

The sheep BAAAAED loudly and began to mutter crossly amongst themselves.

"Who's he calling silly? BAAA!" bleated Shampoo.

"The cheek of it! BAAA!" bleated Shirl.

"We'll show him who's silly, BAAA!" bleated Charmaine.

Gertie opened the gate to the field. Shoo stalked inside and ordered the sheep out. The sheep muttered and shuffled forward.

"Move along," barked Shoo. "No time for gossiping."

The sheep grumbled and scuffed the ground.

"Hurry up, or else!" barked Shoo.

The sheep stopped in their tracks and Shampoo bleated, "NOW!"

Suddenly, they changed direction and ran as fast as they could towards the woods.

"Stop!" barked Shoo. "WOOF!"

But the sheep kept on going. As soon as they reached the woods, they spread out. Some of them went exploring: "Oooo, look at this!" Some of them hid behind trees: "He won't find us here." Some of them found tasty plants to eat: "Yum yum, better than grass."

All of them ignored Shoo, who was crossly barking orders at them from the edge of the woods. "Come back at once! WOOF WOOF WOOF WOOF!"

Shoo crouched down low, he ran this way and that, he crept round in circles, he did everything he had been taught, but the sheep took no notice.

"You can't tell us what to do. We only obey Farmer Larkin," they said.

Just then, Gertie appeared. "Having trouble?" she asked.

"I can't get these silly sheep to come out of the woods," said Shoo. "They're all hiding and laughing at me."

"Have you tried being nice to them?" said Baggy from his field. "No one likes being called silly."

Shoo didn't really feel like being nice, after the trouble the sheep had caused him, but he had to get them back somehow.

"Please, please, will you go back to your field?" said Shoo.

The sheep looked at each other.

"What do you think, girls? Do you think he asked nicely enough?" said Shampoo.

The other sheep nodded their heads.

"Off we go then," said Shirl.

And they stampeded out of the woods, past Shoo, down into their field, where Gertie locked them in just as Farmer Larkin arrived.

"Come on then, Shoo, let's get these sheep down to the barn, and see if you can do it without letting any of them escape this time."

Shoo looked anxiously at the sheep. The sheep looked at each other and winked. When Farmer Larkin whistled, Shoo crouched down low, ran this way and that and crept round in circles. He didn't look at butterflies, he didn't chase rabbits, and he didn't speak to Gertie. For the very first time, he did everything he was told, and the sheep, feeling he had learned his lesson, were happy to follow orders, as long as Shoo spoke to them nicely.

Gertie Sleeps In

There was no doubt about it, Gertie the Goat was naughty. If she could do something she wasn't supposed to do, and it was fun, then she would do it. "I'm still just a young kid at heart," she would tell the other animals when they tutted and said she was old enough to know better.

One day, Gertie did something very naughty indeed.

She waited until the farmhouse was empty, butted the front door open with her head, and went inside!

"I'll just have a little look," she said.

Shoo the Sheepdog watched her go in and couldn't believe his eyes.

"Gertie's gone into the farmhouse!" he told the other animals. He went to look through the window.

"I know she's a bit naughty," said Primrose the Pig, standing up at the wall of her sty, "but that's *very* naughty."

Gertie strolled into the hallway and sniffed around. She was hungry. "I'll just have a little taste of something," she said. She tried the boots by the door, but they were too rubbery. BOING!

The dried flowers on top of the dresser tasted disgusting. YUCK! She opened another door and found a roll of soft pink paper waiting to be chewed. It didn't taste too bad at all, but it made her mouth dry.

Gertie pushed open another door. Dozens of mouth-watering smells curled around her. On the table was a plate piled high with mince pies. YUM! On the hob was a plate of cheese straws. MMM! Next to it was a tray full of home-made chocolates. COR! Gertie sniffed at them one by one and knew that what she was about to do was the naughtiest thing she had ever done.

"I'll just have one or two," she said to herself. With that, she wolfed down two mince pies, five cheese straws and a mouthful of chocolates. SCRUMMY!

"She's eaten some mince pies!" said Shoo.

"Ooooo!" said Primrose.

"That's *soooo* naughty!"

Gertie went back for more, and more. "Stop it, Gertie," she said to herself. "They'll notice."

Shoo's bowl stood in the corner of the kitchen, so she licked that clean instead.

"She's eaten all my food!" said Shoo.

"My, my!" said Primrose. "How naughty can you get?"

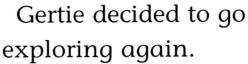

Gertie decided to go exploring again.

"I'll just look in here," she said, opening another door. In the room was a tree covered with shiny balls and coloured ribbons. Gertie tasted the tree and spat it out, YEUK!

But she could smell something delicious hidden among the branches. She sniffed hard and bit into a snowman-shaped decoration. There was chocolate inside. YUM! She yomped it down and looked for more. She found another five, and then saw one hanging right at the top of the tree. She stood on her hind legs and tried to pull it off. She pulled too hard. The tree came crashing down. CRASH!

"She's pulled down the Christmas tree!" said Shoo. "She's in big trouble now."

"Enormous trouble," said Primrose.

Gertie looked at the mess all around her. "Time to go I think."

She ran out into the hall and was about to leave when she saw the staircase. "I wonder what's up there? I'll just have a quick look."

She bounded up the stairs and looked through one of the doors. Behind it was the comfiest-looking sleeping place she had ever seen.

"I must just try it out," said Gertie. She heaved herself up onto the bed and lay down. "MMMMM! So cosy and warm. MMMMMM! I'll just have a quick forty winks."

She was woken by a scream and a very angry voice.

"You naughty, naughty goat," cried Mrs Larkin.

Gertie jumped to her feet, leapt off the bed, bounded down the stairs, out through the door, across the farmyard and into her field. She hid there for the rest of the day, and missed her evening meal. The next day her belly didn't feel at all well. The other animals told her it served her right.

"I know," said Gertie. "It was naughty, very naughty, but I'm just a young kid at heart."